Bears in the Bath

Shirley Parenteau
illustrated by David Walker

Water, soap and
sponge are there.
The bath is ready.
Where are the bears?

Big Brown Bear
calls them in.
His eyes get bigger!
Where have they been?

Eww!

Dust and dirt smudge
Floppy Bear.
Are those cobwebs
in her hair?

Fuzzy Bear
trudges in.
Mud spatters her
from toes to chin!

Now Calico
runs from the yard
with sweaty fur
from playing hard.

What's that smell?
Yellow Bear!
He's stinky and
he doesn't care.

They're reeky, yucky,
GRIMY bears!
Look!
Mud and paw prints
everywhere!

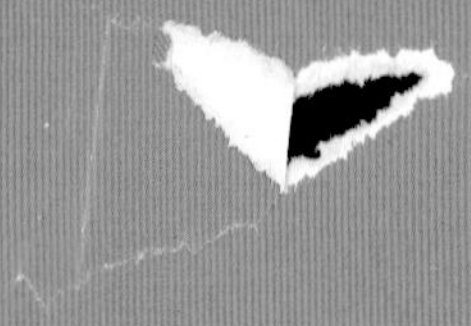

Uh-oh!

Four grungy bears
see the tub
and Big Brown Bear
waiting to scrub.

All four bears
back away.
"We don't want
a bath," they say.

The big bear says,
"You need a scrub!"
He chases them
around the tub.

He scoops up one
and then two more.
He grabs the last.
He's got all four!

They won't go in.
The bears all wriggle.
The more he tries,
the more they giggle!

Oh, no!

Now Big Brown Bear
has smudges and smears
from the tips of his toes
to the tops of his ears!

SPLISH, SPLASH,
SPLOOSH!

He jumps in the tub!
He grabs some soap
and starts to scrub.

He splashes water.
He splashes bears.
He sure is having
fun in there!

Yellow Bear
dives right in!
He piles suds
on Big Bear's chin.

Floppy and Fuzzy
hop over the rim.
Now Calico
gets in with them.

They toss the bubbles.
They giggle and shriek.
Soon each little bear
is clean and sleek.

Yay!

They dry their fur.
What fun it's been!
Now all five bears
are clean again!

For Bill — for sharing life's adventures with me, our children
and now with our grandchildren
S. P.

For every child who would rather play in the mud
than splash in the tub!
D. W.

First published 2016 by Walker Books Ltd
87 Vauxhall Walk, London SE11 5HJ

2 4 6 8 10 9 7 5 3 1

This book was typeset in Journal

Printed in China

British Library Cataloguing in Publication Data:
A catalogue record for this book is available from the British Library

ISBN 978-1-4063-7266-3

www.walker.co.uk